MONSTER HUNTERS
Discover the Thunderbird

by Jan Fields
Illustrated by Scott Brundage

Calico

An Imprint of Magic Wagon
abdobooks.com

abdobooks.com

Published by Magic Wagon, a division of ABDO, PO Box 398166, Minneapolis, Minnesota 55439. Copyright © 2019 by Abdo Consulting Group, Inc. International copyrights reserved in all countries. No part of this book may be reproduced in any form without written permission from the publisher. Calico™ is a trademark and logo of Magic Wagon.

Printed in the United States of America, North Mankato, Minnesota.
102018
012019

THIS BOOK CONTAINS RECYCLED MATERIALS

Written by Jan Fields
Illustrated by Scott Brundage
Edited by Tamara L. Britton
Design Contributors: Candice Keimig & Laura Mitchell

Library of Congress Control Number: 2018947943

Publisher's Cataloging-in-Publication Data

Names: Fields, Jan, author. | Brundage, Scott, illustrator.
Title: Discover the thunderbird / by Jan Fields; illustrated by Scott Brundage.
Description: Minneapolis, Minnesota : Magic Wagon, 2019. | Series: Monster hunters set 3
Summary: The Monster Hunters head to Illinois to investigate the Thunderbird for their Discover Cryptids Internet show. A giant bird reportedly grabbed a kid and flew away! Locals don't believe it. But it's a story the team isn't so quick to dismiss!
Identifiers: ISBN 9781532133671 (lib. bdg.) | ISBN 9781532134272 (ebook) | ISBN 9781532134579 (Read-to-me ebook)
Subjects: LCSH: Monsters--Juvenile fiction. | Legends--Juvenile fiction. | Internet videos--Juvenile fiction.
Classification: DDC [FIC]--dc23

TABLE of CONTENTS

chapter 1

ATTACKED!

Gabe Brown walked along the narrow road. As it headed downhill, it twisted in wide turns like a lazy snake on a hot day. The woods were still. He knew he should be able to hear a car coming long before he saw one, so he walked in the road, near the edge with his best friend Tyler.

As they walked, Gabe swept the woods beside them slowly with the small camera. He turned to Tyler who asked the question that he had clearly been thinking about for a while. "You don't believe in Rebobs, do you?"

"Flying monkeys?" Gabe said looking sideways at his friend. "Not really. It seems a little silly."

The team was in Napa Valley, California, to shoot an episode of *Discover Cryptids* on Rebobs. It was the most unbelievable cryptid story Gabe had ever heard, like something from an old black-and-white movie. In the story, the flying monkeys supposedly escaped from a crazy lab experiment and scared some people going for a drive. For once, Gabe really didn't expect to see anything but trees and birds.

Tyler picked up a small rock from the road and tossed it into the woods. "We should go in there if we really want to find Rebobs. They're probably hiding."

"Because that's what flying monkeys do," Gabe said dryly. "We can't. The forest is private land, and Ben couldn't get permission for us to film there. The owners are tired of people stomping around and leaving litter everywhere."

Tyler stopped walking and stared into the trees. "We wouldn't litter."

"Since when are you so brave anyway?" Gabe asked. "You aren't usually in a hurry to go anywhere that's dark and creepy." He gestured with the camera. "Those woods are both."

Tyler crossed his arms over his chest. "I'm not a chicken."

"I never said you were." Gabe couldn't understand why his friend was acting so weird. Tyler didn't have to be super brave to be a good monster hunter. "We need to focus on shooting video of this road and the edge of the woods as we walk down to meet the van. Ben wants the background footage. The bulk of the episode will be interviews of people talking about this story."

"But what if we went in the woods and got video of actual Rebobs?" Tyler said. "Ben would love that. Ratings would go through the roof."

Gabe doubted that. First, they weren't going to find flying monkeys in the woods. Second,

Discover Cryptids was just a small Internet show. They had some fans, sure. But even if they found flying monkeys, it wasn't likely to put their ratings through the roof. "Come on, let's get down to Ben."

Tyler's expression turned stubborn. "Nope. I'm going to go in the woods. If you don't want to come, I'll take pictures of the Rebobs with my phone."

"Oh, come on," Gabe said. "If we trespass, Ben will be furious. Plus, it's wrong and illegal. We don't have permission. What has gotten into you? We don't do things like that."

They stared at one another for a moment, then Tyler finally said, "Fine. No walking on the posted land."

Gabe picked up the pace, hoping to get to the bottom before Tyler started in again. His friend dragged his feet, falling behind. Gabe sighed. "Look, I don't think you're a chicken. You don't have to prove anything to me. You know that, right? Tyler? Right?"

Gabe turned around, but he didn't see Tyler at all. With a groan, he checked the trees in the woods nearby. At least they'd gotten beyond the no trespassing signs, but Gabe didn't think that made Tyler's actions okay. He cupped his hands around his mouth and bellowed his friend's name. The woods around him seemed to swallow up the sound. Gabe got no answer.

He pulled out his phone and texted Tyler. "Get out of there!"

If Tyler saw the text, he didn't answer. Gabe paced back and forth. He didn't want to go into the woods. Ignoring Ben's directions could get them thrown off the show. What was going on in Tyler's head?

That's when Gabe heard Tyler yell. He sounded terrified. Gabe didn't hesitate. He plunged into the woods, running toward the

yelling as fast as he could. He dodged around trees and jumped over exposed roots. The sound of Tyler's screams died away, and Gabe didn't know if that was good or bad. He suspected it might be bad.

Then just as he scrambled up the side of a thick fallen tree, he saw Tyler running toward him. "Tyler?"

"Rebob!" Tyler yelled as he ran. "It's coming after me."

Gabe saw something was chasing Tyler, but he couldn't tell what. The creature was partially blocked by the brush between Gabe and Tyler. But then he heard the sound of wings flapping. They sounded like big wings.

Tyler hit the side of the tree that Gabe still stood on. Gabe knelt and grabbed Tyler's hand. Hauling him up. "Go!" Tyler yelled. "It's got wings. It can still get us!"

That's when the creature burst through the

brush, flapping its wings and making loud, angry sounds.

Gabe almost screamed. Then his brain sorted out exactly what he was seeing and hearing.

chapter 2

TECH
TROUBLE

"How was I supposed to know it was just a goose?" Tyler demanded, not for the first time. He'd complained about the goose attack across five states.

"You wouldn't have annoyed the goose if you'd stayed out of the woods," Sean said. "Geese are very territorial. And they bite."

"I know," Tyler said, rubbing his rear end through his jeans.

"You deserved the bite," Gabe said, still a bit annoyed at his friend. "You're just lucky you never got onto the posted land. Then you would have been breaking the law."

Tyler crossed his arms over his chest, still glaring. "Look, I said I was sorry."

"Right." Gabe went back to scanning the sky, looking for the drone Sean was flying. He didn't see the drone at all, so he looked over Sean's shoulder at the screen on the controller. "The camera works great."

Sean didn't answer, but Tyler grumbled, "I still don't know why I'm not the one flying the drone. I do the tech. It's my thing."

"You are also excitable," Sean said calmly. "And prone to screaming and running."

"I am not!" Tyler insisted. "I only run when the situation calls for it. And I hardly ever scream."

"Sure," Sean said, then he muttered under his breath. "Goose boy."

"I'm sure you would have stayed totally calm if you'd known it was a goose chasing you," Gabe said, hoping to calm his friend down. They were lucky Ben had thought the goose incident was funny, though they'd both gotten lectures on following directions. Now they needed to focus on the next job and prove they were dependable. "Remember, Ben said Sean had to run the drone. It's not ours. It's only on loan from a potential sponsor for our Thunderbird episode. Breaking it would be bad, and Sean has steadier hands."

"I don't break things," Tyler grumbled, crossing his arms over his chest. "Name one piece of tech I've broken. Ben's just mad at me."

And for good reason, Gabe thought, though he had to admit that what Tyler had said was true. He had never broken any of the equipment he handled. He also did a fantastic job of keeping track of all the bits and bobs they needed for shooting *Discover Cryptids*.

Gabe knew that he, Tyler, and Sean were lucky Gabe's brother Ben needed them to help on the show. How many kids got to travel all over looking for monsters?

"So what would you do if we actually spotted

a Thunderbird?" Sean asked.

Tyler drew himself up very straight and said, "I would carefully record footage of it for the series, but I don't know how Thunderbirds could live here. You couldn't exactly hide." He gestured at the nearly flat land around them. It was spotted with trees but was really more farmland than anything. Not only did the flat land mean they could see far into the distance, it also made the sky seem bigger than Gabe had ever seen it.

"Thunderbirds don't live here," Sean said. "They couldn't. There isn't sufficient food supply for a giant bird. But my research suggests they pass over parts of Illinois while migrating."

"If they exist at all," Gabe added.

"Actually, Thunderbirds are one of the more likely cryptids," Sean said, never taking his eyes from the controls. "They are probably teratorns."

Tyler's frown deepened. "Huh?"

"Teratorns are giant birds that are supposedly extinct," Sean said. "Teratorns in Argentina were said to be as tall as a person and have a twenty-five foot wingspan."

Tyler grumbled. "I think people would notice birds that big."

"People have," Gabe said. "That's why we're in Illinois."

"In one report, a bird grabbed a kid our age and almost flew off with him," Sean said and Gabe winced. That was one detail Tyler didn't need to know.

"It grabbed a kid our age?" Tyler echoed, his voice a high squeak.

Sean blinked at him. "That's what I said." Then he pointed at the clouds, which had crept closer while they talked. "Thunderbird sightings also tend to occur when storms are nearby. I believe the birds use the wind to help them fly."

"Lucky for the birds," Tyler muttered.

Sean ignored him. "This is probably why Illinois is the most common location for Thunderbird sightings. The state is known for its wide variety of weather, including huge winter storms, tornadoes, and vicious heat waves."

Tyler hunched his shoulders and watched the sky. "Should we be out here? A storm could crash the drone."

"Tyler has a point," Gabe said.

"All the more reason to practice in harsh conditions," Sean answered, not looking up from the controls.

"Yeah, but it also means the drone could be hit by lightning." Gabe pointed at the controller. "So bring it in."

Sean looked at him for a long moment, but then sighed and said, "Fine." He began to fiddle with the controls, his attention split between the controller and the sky.

A huge shadow passed over the area, throwing them into gloom. Tyler shrieked, "A Thunderbird!" He took off for the van.

His eyes still on the sky, Sean stepped into Tyler's path.

They slammed into one another. The controller flew out of Sean's hands. Gabe dove for it, catching it just before it hit the ground. "I got it."

And that's when the drone itself slammed into the field with a crunching sound that made Gabe feel sick.

chapter 3

COUSIN
ISAAC

Ben ran from the van when he heard Tyler screaming. Gabe held his breath as his brother gently picked up the drone. He stared at it in horror.

It didn't take a tech genius to see that crashing had done damage, lots of damage. Ben looked at Sean. "What happened?"

"Tyler ran into me," Sean said. "I dropped the controller."

"Something flew over us," Tyler insisted. "Something big."

Ben frowned. "What kind of something?"

"I don't know," Sean said. "I didn't see it before Tyler ran over me, and I dropped the controller." He glared at Tyler. "He probably just saw the shadow thrown from the drone."

"That's not true!" Tyler looked at Ben and snapped his mouth shut. Gabe could tell by the expression on his brother's face that Ben did not want to hear Tyler's excuses. For once, Tyler saw the same thing.

"I caught it," Gabe said hopefully, holding up the controller. Ben's gaze turned to him and the hope drained right out of Gabe. "But I didn't catch it quickly enough."

"This was going to be a major sponsorship," Ben said as he cradled the drone gently. "More money. More equipment. More viewers." He looked down at the drone and stopped talking.

Tyler cleared his throat. "I might have an answer."

Gabe's breath caught again. This was not the time for Tyler to come up with an idea.

Ben narrowed his eyes. "What?"

"I have a cousin," Tyler said. "He lives near

here. He's kind of a tech genius. He could probably fix the drone."

"He lives in Illinois?" Ben asked.

Tyler bobbed his head. "Lawndale."

Sean snapped to attention. "Lawndale is where the Thunderbird grabbed that kid."

Tyler swallowed hard. "Isaac's family only moved to Illinois last year, so they probably don't know anything about the Thunderbird, but if anyone can fix the drone, it's Isaac."

Ben looked at him for a long moment, then said, "Everyone in the van. Tyler, you call your cousin. We'll go see what kind of tech genius he really is." Gabe suspected this might be Tyler's last chance.

Gabe stared out the window as they drove on quiet roads by neat, one-story homes and carefully tended lawns with very few trees. They also passed lots and lots of cornfields.

No one spoke, which was strange. Usually

Sean would be calling out facts about Illinois and Tyler would argue with him about half of them.

All the quiet made Gabe's stomach hurt. *Isaac better be able to fix the drone*, Gabe thought. He wanted things back to normal. "It sure is flat here," he said.

"The great plains are flatter and more open," Sean said, clearly unable to resist the temptation to spout facts. "Illinois is known for its agricultural productivity."

"Mostly corn by the look of it," Gabe said, hoping to keep the facts flowing. Just hearing Sean talk made him feel a little better.

"Corn and soybeans make up the bulk of the crops grown," Sean said. "Though the state is also known for its hogs, cattle, and dairy products."

"Like cheese?" Tyler asked, sounding cheerful for the first time.

Ben's flat voice cut through the conversation. "This is Main Street, Lawndale." The remark made everyone in the van jump since Ben hadn't spoken in miles.

Gabe looked out the window at some huge buildings shaped like cylinders. His curiosity overcame his worries about Ben's mood. "What are those?"

"Grain Elevators," Sean said. "Probably to store all the corn grown around here. Did you know, the round Silo for farm storage of animal feed was first constructed on a farm in Spring Grove, Illinois?"

Gabe felt his tense muscles begin to relax at the familiar sound of Sean showing off. Right up until Ben interrupted again, his voice still tight, "We're almost there. I hope your cousin is as good as you say, Tyler."

Tyler looked at Gabe, and Gabe knew his friend hoped so too.

The van pulled into a short, empty driveway that led to an equally empty carport. The small house attached to the carport was a sunny shade of yellow with bright white trim. "Is anyone home?" Ben asked.

"Just Isaac," Tyler said. "I texted him, and he said he's in the shed outside. He's working on something for a tech competition. I hope he has time to help."

No one responded to that, and Gabe felt the tension in the van crank up again.

They followed Tyler around the house. "Isaac!" he yelled.

The slightly crooked door on a small metal shed stood open, and a teenaged boy walked out. He looked a lot like Tyler, though about six inches taller. Isaac wore his sandy blond hair a little longer than Tyler and freckles splashed across his face, but there was a clear family resemblance. "Hey," he said as he stopped and rocked on his toes.

"Hey." Tyler introduced Ben, Gabe, and Sean.

Ben held out a hand. "Pleased to meet you. I hope you can help with our drone."

Isaac looked at Ben's hand in surprise, but then shook it. "Sure. Where is it?"

"In the van." He gave Gabe a pointed look.

"I'll go get it," Gabe offered, then turned and ran for the van.

While Isaac looked the drone over, Gabe felt his insides churning. Would he be able to fix it? Or were things just going to get worse?

Finally Tyler's cousin said, "This is a nice drone. You guys need to be careful with it."

Before anyone could comment on that, Tyler spoke in a hopeful voice. "Can you fix it?"

Isaac shrugged. "Sure. No problem. I can have it done by tonight sometime, probably. I've got a lot of stuff to work with because of a project I'm working on."

Everyone let out a breath in an audible rush. Ben actually laughed. "We appreciate it. And I'll pay, of course. Tyler said you've been working on something for a competition, so I appreciate you taking time to help us."

Isaac looked at Tyler sharply. "The competition is a secret. Another guy from around here is working on something too. It's all top secret."

"That's all right," Ben assured him. "We won't try to learn your secrets. I'm just glad you think you can fix the drone."

Isaac bobbed his head. He pointed at the words on the side of the van. "I watch *Discover Cryptids* sometimes. My mom likes it too. You here to see the Thunderbird?"

"Not likely," Sean said. "Since the last reported Thunderbird sighting around here was in the 1970s."

"The seventies?" Isaac said with a bark of laughter. "Some guys saw it just last week."

chapter 4

RECENT
SIGHTING

After gaping at Isaac for a long moment, everyone started asking questions at once until Ben held up a hand to stop the noise. He looked directly at Isaac. "How do you know about this?"

Isaac shrugged again. "I go to school with some of the guys who saw it. They don't talk about it much though, so I don't really know the details."

"Do you believe them?" Ben asked.

"I believe they saw something," Isaac said. "They're good guys. They wouldn't make it up for attention. In fact, they don't want attention. They know most people don't believe them."

"But we would," Ben said. "At the very least, we'd give them a fair hearing. Do you think we could talk to them? They could be very helpful."

Isaac winced. "They might not want to talk to you. People think it's stupid to believe in the Thunderbird."

"Tell them we won't think they're stupid," Ben said. "And we won't reveal their names. They can be completely off the record."

"I'll tell them, but I can't make any promises." Isaac hefted the drone in his hands. "Let me take this back to my workshop." He turned to Tyler then. "Mom said to ask if you guys were going to stay here."

"We'll probably get a room at the closest hotel," Ben said. "Can you give me directions?"

"Sure." Isaac laughed. "But it won't be very close. No hotel, no cute country inns, no motels even. We have a campground if you don't mind pitching tents, but it's not that close."

"We have tents," Ben said. He waved a hand toward the backyard. "Would your folks be all right with us pitching them out here?"

"I'll ask. And I'll call the guys who saw the Thunderbird. Let me set this down."

Ben started to follow Isaac into the shed, but Isaac turned at the door and blocked his way. "Sorry," he said. "My competition project is in here."

Ben held up his hands. "Right. No problem. I'll wait out here." He turned around and leaned against the shed.

Sean leaned close to whisper to Tyler. "Looks like coming to see your cousin might be your best idea ever."

Tyler mumbled, "I hope so." He turned to look at Gabe. "Because I think your brother might dump me off right here if Isaac can't fix that drone."

"Ben wouldn't do that," Gabe insisted.

Tyler didn't look like he believed him.

Isaac's friends agreed to talk to them, but only if they promised not to spread their names around. Ben promised quickly enough. "Okay," Isaac said, handing over a scrap of paper. "This is the address for John Morrison. The other guys are hanging out at his house, so they'll meet you there."

They practically ran to the van, and Gabe

sat next to Ben in the front of the van. Since his brother still wasn't talking, Gabe stared out the window. The yards they passed were small and featured mostly close-cropped grass and the occasional lawn gnome. The houses were all single story with simple lines and bright white trim. "Everything around here kind of looks alike," he said.

Sean spoke from a seat behind him, "Though many of the houses do follow the same basic design, they differ in a variety of ways."

Because he knew Sean would happily list all the ways, Gabe quickly called back, "Got it. Thanks." He dropped his voice so it wouldn't carry to the back. "I can still see how someone might make up a giant bird just for something interesting and different to talk about."

"If that were the case," Ben said, "I would expect them to want the attention of being filmed."

"Not if the whole thing has gotten out of control," Gabe said. "Maybe they never expected people to insult them about it."

"Maybe," his brother said. "But I'll keep an open mind until we meet these guys. The story of the Thunderbird in this area is very old."

Sean must have changed seats so he could hear them talk despite Gabe's dropped voice because he spoke from practically right behind Gabe's ear. "Theories about the Thunderbird include it being an Andean condor or a great blue heron. They are both large birds with impressive wingspans."

"But neither of those could pick up a kid my size," Gabe said, twisting around in his seat as much as he could with the seat belt on.

"No," Sean agreed, "but the story of the attack is unique. No one else claimed to have been attacked by the Thunderbird. Most people simply report large birds flying. And with so few trees around here, you don't have much available to judge scale if you look up and spot a bird. So someone might mistakenly believe the bird is bigger than it is."

"Does that mean you don't believe a Thunderbird really grabbed a kid?" Tyler asked, and Gabe was glad to hear his friend joining in. He was worried about how quiet Tyler had been overall since the drone broke.

"I don't know," Sean admitted. "I doubt even a very large bird could fly away with a kid our age. It is possible it was flying down to grab something the boy was holding, and its talons were caught in the kid's clothes."

"I had considered that," Ben said. "The boy's aunt said she fought the bird off, which suggests the boy was still close to the ground if not on it. She may have knocked the bird's talons loose from the boy's clothes."

"Wow," Tyler said, and Gabe heard him flop

back in his seat, "the idea of a giant bird's sharp claws caught in my clothes isn't scary at all."

"Keep in mind that it only happened once," Gabe reminded him.

"Once that we heard about," Sean added in a hopeful voice. "But who knows what could happen if there's still a Thunderbird about here."

"So you'd like to be grabbed by the Thunderbird?" Tyler asked.

"It would give me a chance to observe it close up," Sean said. "But I'd rather you were grabbed, and Gabe filmed it. Then I could view the evidence over and over."

"Thanks pal," Tyler grumbled.

Gabe wasn't thrilled with Sean's idea either, but he was happy that the tone in the van seemed almost normal again. Now if it could just stay that way.

chapter 5

INTO THE CORN

When they finally pulled up before a house that looked a lot like all the others, a group of teenagers piled out the front door, pointing at the van as they walked toward them.

Ben came around the front of the van to shake their hands. Three boys about Isaac's age slouched over, followed by a girl with long dark hair. They mumbled their names as Ben introduced himself.

"We don't want our pictures taken," one boy said. Gabe was pretty sure it was John, though he'd mumbled so low that it could have been Don.

Ben held up his hands. "No pictures. I'd like to record your story though, just so we can go over it later when I write the script for the show. But a digital voice recording only and we won't put the recording on the show."

The teenagers looked at him silently for a long moment, then muttered amongst themselves. Finally, the boy who might be John said, "Okay."

Ben gave Tyler a look, and Tyler ducked back into the van to get the small digital recorder. "Why do you want to keep this secret?" he asked.

"Everyone around here knows about the family that told their story," John said, hunching his shoulders and looking miserable.

"It's a big joke," the girl added. "Everyone laughs at them. I used to laugh too."

Another boy spoke, his voice louder than the others. "We don't want to be a joke, so we don't talk about it. We only told Isaac because he's super smart. We thought he might know what kind of bird it really was."

"Isaac doesn't know about birds," Tyler yelled

from inside the van. "He knows about tech."

The teenager shrugged. "Yeah, he didn't know. But he didn't laugh either, so he's okay."

"Isaac understands." Tyler climbed back out of the van and handed the recorder to Ben. "Nobody wants to be a joke." He sounded serious as he spoke, and Gabe wondered if Sean's teasing might have hurt Tyler more than any of them realized.

"Do you have a place we can sit and talk?"

"We could walk out where we saw the bird," the girl said. "It's not far." She pointed behind the house where a cornfield stretched into the near distance.

"You saw a giant bird in the cornfield?" Sean asked.

The girl shook her head. "On the other side."

"Sounds good," Ben told her.

The teens turned together to head across the yard toward the cornfield. "Watch out for snakes," John said, looking down at his feet.

"Snakes?" Tyler yelped, jumping as if he thought there might already be a snake underfoot.

The teenager looked over his shoulder at them. "Snakes like cornfields because they draw mice."

Tyler didn't say anything else, but he dropped back so he was walking beside Gabe. "I don't like snakes," he said.

"They are scared of you too," Gabe said, hoping it was true. "Just watch where you walk."

As they walked between the rows of corn, Gabe thought about how creepy the cornfield was. All around them, the breeze made the stalks rustle. It sounded as if something crept through the corn alongside them, though Gabe knew that was just his imagination running wild.

Beside him, Tyler walked with his head down, clearly watching for snakes. His gaze darted from the ground in front of his feet to the edges of the rows where the rustling corn lay shadows on the dry ground. "Do snakes chase people?" he asked.

"I don't think so," Gabe said. "But I don't really know. I expect Sean knows."

Tyler shuddered. "I do not want to hear any terrifying snake facts from Sean right now."

Gabe had to agree with that. Sean knew scary facts about nearly everything. Gabe sometimes wondered if researching the worst that could possibly happen actually made it easier for Sean to face things in real life. No matter what tried to bite them or trample them, Sean knew something that could have been worse.

He was still thinking about this when Tyler grabbed his arm and pointed. "I hear something over there."

"I hear something from every cornstalk," Gabe said. "Who knew the country was so noisy?"

"Shh. Not the corn. Something big."

Then Gabe heard it too. Something was definitely pushing through the corn beside them. Something big.

chapter 6

SCARY BIRDS

Before Tyler and Gabe could bolt down the row, a huge black head thrust through the corn and a sharp beak pointed right at them. As the bird pushed through the corn, Tyler shrieked and ran. His yelling clearly startled the bird every bit as much as the bird had scared them. Gabe stood frozen as the huge bird beat massive black wings and seemed to lunge right for Gabe.

With a yelp, Gabe threw himself to the ground, and the black bird leapt into the air, passing through the spot Gabe had stood only moments before. He rolled over to watch it beat its wings and climb into the air.

That's when Gabe realized he must have just seen a crow. "Wow," he whispered. "They look smaller and a lot less scary on TV."

He scrambled to his feet and brushed at the dirt on his clothes as he headed down the corn row. Soon he spotted an opening that led to a cleared piece of dusty ground that didn't seem to be growing anything more than a few scattered weeds.

In the clearing, Tyler was trying to drag Ben back toward the corn. "Come on! Gabe's in there, if the Thunderbird didn't carry him off and eat him."

Gabe walked out of the row, still beating dust off his clothes. "It wasn't the Thunderbird. I think it might have been a crow."

"Oh, come on," Tyler said, throwing his arms wide. "It was huge! Crows aren't that big." Then he paused and added, "I don't think they're that big. Are they?"

Sean cocked his head to look at them curiously. "How big was it?"

"Well, it took off and flew right over me. I think its wingspan might have been longer than I am. And it had a big beak. I wouldn't want it pecking me. It would hurt. A lot."

"That sounds like a common raven," Sean said. "It can have a wingspan of more than fifty inches. Did it have a wedge-shaped tail? A raven has a wedge-shaped tail." He sighed deeply. "I could show you pictures if I had my computer and an Internet connection."

"I don't need to see pictures," Gabe said. "I saw all of it I wanted when I was on the ground, trying not to get pecked to death. But I wasn't looking at its tail. I was looking at its beak and claws."

"Talons," Sean said.

John huffed, clearly beginning to be annoyed by the conversation. "Does it matter?

We get ravens around here sometimes." He lifted his shoulders in a shrug. "It wouldn't peck you to death. It's not a big deal."

"It was a big deal to me," Tyler muttered.

"The bird we saw out here was bigger than a raven," the girl said, stepping up beside John. "We've seen ravens all our lives. This was huge."

"Maybe you saw a turkey vulture," Sean suggested. "That can have wingspans of up to seventy-two inches."

"We've seen those all our lives too," John said. "The Thunderbird was bigger. As big as a small airplane."

"Maybe not quite that big," the girl added, getting a glare from John for contradicting him.

"No living bird is the size of an airplane," Sean said. "Did the bird make a noise? Sometimes a bird can be identified by its call." He then tilted his head back and shrieked, making them all jump. "That was the call of a Swainson's Hawk. They normally live farther west, but they're quite large with a wide wingspan."

Ben held up a hand. "Okay, enough with the bird calls. Why don't you guys just tell us what you saw?"

The teenagers looked at one another for a moment, then John nudged the girl. "You tell them, Emily."

Emily wrapped her arms around herself. "We were out here just hanging around after supper. We all live close by. The guys were throwing a football, pretty badly actually."

The boys objected to that, but she just waved them off. "Anyway, it was getting dark early. I remember I wondered if it might be going to rain, because it was so shadowy."

"I don't remember hearing any strange bird calls," one of the boys said. "But someone was running a lawn mower around here, so it might have drowned out the bird."

"Thomas is right," John said. "I remember thinking the guy was trying to get the lawn mowed before the rain."

"It was all pretty normal," Thomas said.

"Right up until we saw the big shadow. With the clouds, we didn't think about the dark shadow at first," Emily said. "Until I looked up."

"And screamed," Thomas said. "We had no idea Emily could scream like that. It was epic."

"Well, I'd never seen a monster before." She took a step forward and pointed at Ben. "And it was a monster. The wingspan was huge, like ten feet maybe. Maybe more."

"What kind of feathers did it have?" Sean asked. "And what was the shape of the tail feathers? Did you see its beak?"

She glared at him. "I didn't see stuff like that. It moved fast and kind of blended in with the clouds. But it was the biggest bird I'd ever seen. I bet it was the biggest bird anyone has ever seen."

chapter 7
WITNESSES

Though Ben asked the teens more questions, it was clear they'd gotten all the details anyone remembered. The bird was huge and fast. Anything else, they simply didn't know.

"And you haven't seen it since?" Ben asked, pointing the digital recorder at the group.

The teens all shook their heads. They all looked very distressed. John exchanged looks with his friends, then added, "We haven't come out here since then until now. We don't want to see it."

"We're not scared," one of the boys insisted as he shoved his hands into his pockets. "But that doesn't mean we want to see something like that again."

Ben gestured toward the ground. "Do you know who owns this piece of land?"

Emily bobbed her head. "My uncle." She pointed past the clearing toward a patch of woods. "He owns the woods there too, and his house is on the other side. He used to farm this piece of land too but he's kind of old now."

"Do you think he'd let us camp here?"

"Why would we want to do that?" Tyler asked, kicking at a dry dirt clod.

"If this is a migratory route for the Thunderbird," Sean said. "It may pass over again."

"And grab someone." Tyler waved his hands around. "It did that once, remember?"

Emily waited until Tyler was done ranting, then pulled a cell phone out of her pocket, "Uncle Joe wouldn't mind if you stayed. I'm sure of it, and I can ask him if you want."

Ben offered her a smile. "Thanks! That would

be great. I appreciate your help."

Tyler flopped onto the ground muttering about how they needed to keep low to make themselves harder to grab.

After Emily talked for a few minutes, she turned to Ben with a thumbs-up as she thanked her uncle and ended the call. "He says it's fine as long as you guys don't leave a mess. You can have a campfire if you're careful, but you'll have to buy firewood. He says there's nothing growing on this piece of land to burn."

"We won't need a fire," Ben assured her. "And we'll leave the land just like we found it."

The teens moved toward the cornfield, clearly eager to be gone from the area. John gave Ben an apologetic look at he edged away. "I'll ask my parents if you can use our bathroom if you need to. Mom won't mind, for sure. You can just come and knock on the back door."

"Thanks." Ben turned to Gabe, Sean, and

Tyler. "We'd better go get our camping stuff out of the van and get set up."

"I think it would be best if I stay with Tyler's cousin," Sean suggested. "I'll have computer access there, and I can work on editing video."

Gabe put his hands on his hips and stared at his friend. "We haven't shot anything that needs editing."

Sean spread his own hands, palms up. "I want to be prepared."

"You just want to get out of being attacked by a giant bird," Tyler grumbled.

"Actually, he probably wants to skip out on sleeping in a sleeping bag," Gabe countered.

"I do find I work better indoors," Sean admitted.

"Forget it," Ben said as he turned toward the cornfield and started walking. "We stay together. Let's go."

As they walked back through the rows of corn stalks, Tyler poked Sean in the arm. "If anyone was staying with my cousin, it would be me," he whispered.

"No one is staying behind," Ben called out. "We're going to watch for the Thunderbird together." Then he stopped suddenly. "Do you think your cousin will have the drone done yet?"

Tyler gave him a doubtful look as he pulled a phone out of his pocket. "That would be really fast, even for Isaac." He looked down at the phone. "I'm not getting a signal right here."

"Check again when we get out of the field," Ben suggested.

Tyler shoved the phone back in his pocket and trudged along behind Ben, looking completely miserable.

Gabe dropped back to walk beside Tyler. "Don't worry. We'll be in a tent. Even a Thunderbird couldn't pick us all up at one time."

"No, but some of the time we'll be out in the field," Sean said cheerfully. "And given a choice, the bird would almost certainly go for Tyler." He pointed at Tyler's blond hair. "That color mimics the light-colored fur of rabbits, which would likely be a prey item for the bird."

Tyler quickly covered his head with his hands as he looked up into the sky. He ran ahead to walk close beside Ben. Ben looked down at Tyler's hunched shoulders and the hands on his head and shook his head without speaking.

Gabe glared at Sean. "You did that on purpose," he said.

Sean shrugged. "It's true." Then he called out loud enough for Tyler to hear. "Some chickens are that color too. I'm sure a big, meat-eating bird would just love some tasty chicken!"

Tyler just hunched over more as they trudged the rest of the way through the cornfield.

chapter 8

SETTING THE SNARE

When they reached the van, the boys started to scramble for the tent bags and backpacks, but Ben called them back. "I've changed my mind," Ben said. "We'll head to Isaac's house and check on his progress with the drone and get some suggestions of where we could go for supper. Isaac can probably tell us what we can find available close by, even if it's just hot dogs from a convenience store."

Tyler perked up at that. "I do like hot dogs."

As it turned out, their return to Isaac's house was full of good news. Isaac had fixed the drone, and his mom insisted they stay and eat supper. When they smelled fried chicken, the grins on their faces stretched wide.

The inside of the house was as tidy and bright as the outside, with white walls and neat blue curtains on the windows. Isaac's mom sent Tyler and Isaac to the hall closet to retrieve some folding chairs so there would be places for everyone around the table. As it was, they had to tuck in their elbows to fit, but it was well worth it.

"I've watched a few episodes of your show," Isaac's mom said as she passed the mashed potatoes to Ben. "I found it very interesting."

"A little silly though," Isaac's dad said. "Seems like you could put all that energy into investigating something real."

Sean set his chicken leg back on his plate. "Many people believe cryptids are real. The legends sometimes go back hundreds of years or more."

"Some folks believe in ghosts too," Isaac's dad said. "Still don't make 'em real."

Ben scooped potatoes onto his plate. "We aren't really interested in proving them real, though that would be great. We're interested in the stories and the people who tell them. In many places, cryptids are a huge part of the local lore and even help with the local economy."

Isaac's dad stared at Ben. "How does that work?"

"Towns hold festivals and sell souvenirs. Some have museums dedicated to the local legends," Ben said. "Some even put up statues."

"Kooks," Isaac's dad said.

Isaac cleared his throat to pull attention away from cryptids. "You should probably test the drone this evening. Then, if it's acting wonky, you can bring it back and I'll work on it some more."

Gabe appreciated the change of topic. He didn't like it when people talked down the show. He knew *Discover Cryptids* was really important to Ben. "There should be plenty of room in the clearing before we pitch the tents," he said.

"Can I drive the drone?" Tyler asked.

Gabe held his breath, thinking his friend was really pushing his luck. Even Sean looked surprised by the question. Ben turned his attention to Tyler but didn't speak immediately. He tapped his fork lightly against his pile of mashed potatoes.

"Look," Tyler said. "I wasn't flying the drone when it crashed. And I'm normally the one who handles the tech. We have no way of knowing if it would have crashed if I'd been flying it."

Sean sat up very straight, scowling at Tyler. "I was flying it perfectly well."

"You were," Gabe agreed, hoping to defuse the situation. "But if Tyler had been concentrating on flying the drone, it might have made a difference."

Sean grumbled, but Ben nodded slowly. "You

have valid points. And since we have Isaac to fix it if necessary, I suppose it would be fine for Tyler to fly the drone today. After that, I'll decide who should be in charge of it."

The smile that bloomed on Tyler's face swept away the tension in Gabe's stomach. He did think it might be a good idea to change the subject before Ben had a chance to change his mind. He looked at Isaac, "So how is your secret project coming?"

"I hope it'll be done soon," Isaac's dad grumbled. "I'd like to be able to put my lawn mower back in the shed."

"I wouldn't have had to take over the shed if Mom let me work in the house," Isaac said.

"Not after the fire you started in your room," his mom replied. "I thought we'd never get that smell out of the house."

Sean scooped some peas onto his fork. "What are the parameters of the competition?"

he asked. "Are you inventing something new?"

Isaac shook his head. "We aren't trying to invent new tech. We're recreating existing machines using only recycled or reclaimed materials. Imagine making a food processor from trash. That's the idea. My piece will come in very handy around here."

His parents both looked slightly alarmed at that. "I don't really need a food processor made from trash, dear," his mother said.

"Good," Isaac said. "Because that's not what I made. I made something way more useful."

"And you said you know someone else around the area who is competing?" Ben asked.

Isaac bobbed his head. "Stephen Berger, but his entry won't be anything useful. It never is. He just goes for big and flashy. Last year he made a parade float that drives itself. Who needs that?"

"When is this competition going to be judged?" Ben asked.

"At the end of the month," Isaac answered, taking a sip of his iced tea.

"Good," his dad said. "I'm looking forward to it. And so is my lawn mower."

Isaac's mother gave him a nervous smile. "I'm looking forward to seeing what you made too, dear. I'm sure it'll be wonderful."

Gabe suspected none of what she just said was true, and it made him wonder just what kinds of weird creations Tyler's cousin normally made.

When supper was over, Ben insisted they stay to help with dishes, and Isaac's mother beamed at them as they cleaned up. Of course Sean managed to get out of helping by insisting he needed to take advantage of the Internet connection while they had it. "Since you plan for us to sleep out in the wilds tonight."

Isaac's mother laughed. "Joe Morrison's backyard isn't exactly the wilds."

Ben leaned close to the kitchen window as he washed. "Looks like it's clouding up. I hope it's not going to rain on us."

Sean looked up from where he was at the kitchen table with his laptop out. "That would be horrible." He quickly tapped on some keys on the computer then said, "The weather report says cloudy but only a twenty percent chance of rain."

Ben handed a dish to Gabe. "We should be fine then."

As Gabe dried it, he remembered that the teens said it was cloudy when they saw the Thunderbird. Then he shrugged it off. There's no way that would make any difference, right?

chapter 9

TYLER
THE HERO

When they returned to John's house the clouds were thick in the sky. John waved at them from his yard, but didn't come any closer. Instead, he shoved his hands into the pockets of his hoodie and slouched down the street.

Ben began piling camping things onto Gabe and Sean while Tyler stood nearby carrying the drone as if it might shatter under his grip. Sean glared in Tyler's direction as he hefted a backpack onto his shoulder. Usually it was Sean who managed to get away with not carrying anything. Tyler just beamed back at Sean.

"You guys head to the clearing and set up the tents," Ben said. "I know the weather report said only twenty percent chance of rain, but I still think we should have a roof over our heads as soon as possible."

"When are we going to try out the drone?" Tyler asked eagerly.

"Tents first," Ben insisted. "Then drone. And I'm going to catch up with Isaac. I have something I want to ask him." He hefted another item into Gabe's arms and the boys headed for the cornfield.

The cloudy skies deepened the shadows between the rows of corn, making the cornfield extra creepy. Gabe couldn't walk fast under the load of camping gear, but he was much faster than Sean who had to make frequent stops to complain about the weight and rearrange his load. Since he was carrying the lighter weight, Tyler soon trotted so far ahead that Gabe couldn't even see him.

With the growing distance between the boys, Gabe felt alone in the rustling corn. He had to keep reminding himself that it just felt like that. It wasn't really like that. When he finally reached the clearing, he was glad to hear someone mowing the lawn in the distance. It made him feel less isolated.

Gabe dumped the bags and packs on the ground next to Tyler. "You're going to have to put down the drone long enough to help pitch the tents."

Tyler reluctantly put the drone down. "Where's Sean?"

"Probably sitting out in the middle of the cornfield waiting for Ben to come and carry part of the gear. We have one tent though so we can get started."

As they began pulling the tent out of the bag, Gabe realized the sound of the lawn mower was getting closer. "Do you hear that?"

"You mean the lawn mower?" Tyler asked as he gave the tent another yank. "Yeah, of course."

Gabe looked around the clearing. "Why would it be coming closer? You don't suppose someone is going to try to mow this clearing with us in it."

That's when Tyler screamed. Gabe spun to look at him. Tyler stared wild-eyed into the sky and pointed. Gabe looked up as a huge shadow passed over them, and Gabe spotted the silhouette of a bird, the biggest bird he'd ever seen. And it was flying right at them!

Gabe forced his attention away from the sky and grabbed the small camera bag. He had to film this!

The lawn mower sounded like it was right on top of them as the bird flew over and then vanished into the gathering darkness. "The Thunderbird," Tyler yelled. "And we didn't get a single picture."

"Maybe you could chase it with the drone," Gabe suggested. He'd gotten the camera from the bag and held it uselessly. "There was something really strange about that bird."

Tyler ran to the drone and grabbed the controller. "I'll see if the drone can find it."

Gabe realized the lawn mower sound was getting louder again. And Tyler yelled, "It's coming back."

The giant bird appeared from nowhere, but this time it was flying much, much lower. "Look out!" Tyler yelled. "It's coming after you."

No, Gabe thought as he stared at the giant bird silhouette and raised his camera. *It's not*.

But before Gabe could gather his thoughts to answer Tyler, his friend had run toward him yelling. "Get away from my friend!"

Tyler launched the drone, sending it straight for the swiftly approaching Thunderbird. The bird veered off sharply, but it also lost even more altitude. Gabe knew then what he was seeing. It wasn't a bird. It was a plane.

The pilot of the ultralight must have been struggling with the controls as the plane jerked, and stalled. It then came down in the clearing, hitting the ground somewhere between a landing and a crash.

At nearly the same moment, Ben and Sean burst out of the cornfield, shouting in surprise. Tyler landed the drone and joined them as they

Though it took a while for the whole story to come out, Sean was the first to guess that the ultralight was part of the competition Isaac was in. "You're Stephen Berger, aren't you?"

The man bobbed his head. "Yeah, I was borrowing the Thunderbird legend to keep my contest entry secret while I tested it." He winced as he looked at his plane. "Now I'll be lucky if I can get this thing running again by the time of the competition."

"You know, someone could have been hurt by your actions," Ben said. "You're lucky."

"Yeah, I guess so," Stephen said sheepishly. "I didn't exactly think it through."

Then Tyler grinned at everyone. "On the other hand, I got some fantastic footage of the Thunderbird."

Stephen looked around at Ben and the boys. "You guys have to keep this a secret. I don't want word of this getting out before the competition."

"How about after the competition?" Ben asked.

Stephen smiled. "Then it would be fine. In fact, it would be great!"

Gabe shot a quick video of Ben interviewing Stephen, then they helped him find all the parts of the plane that had broken off in the crash landing. Finally, Stephen called for a trailer to haul his plane home. "I'll cover it up with a few tarps, and it can stay secret."

"Not completely secret," Ben said. "I think the teenagers you scared have a right to know too."

Stephen reluctantly agreed.

Since they'd never set up the tents, Ben said they could pack up and find a hotel since they wouldn't be looking for the Thunderbird in the field any more. Gabe and Tyler loaded up on vending machine treats on the way to the rooms. Ben pointed at them. "Don't make yourselves

sick. We'll be up early to shoot the interviews with John and his friends."

"They don't have to worry about anyone thinking they were lying now," Gabe said. "And we have the drone footage to prove it."

Sean patted his laptop. "Footage I'll be editing as soon as we get in the room."

Ben laughed. "Junk food and video editing. You boys know how to have a good time."

"Tyler deserves all the junk food he wants," Gabe said. "He ran right into danger to save me."

Sean rolled his eyes. "From a homemade ultralight airplane."

"He didn't know that," Gabe reminded him. "And that makes him a hero to me."

Tyler blushed but he didn't argue.

Once they got settled in the room, they all crowded around the single tiny desk and watched the video before Sean started to work

on it. "Hey, pause that," Ben said. "Run it back."

Sean paused the video, then started it forward frame by frame. Since Tyler had been mostly trying to drive the Thunderbird off before it could grab Gabe, the footage swung wildly more than once. It was during one of those swings that Ben stabbed the screen with his finger. "What's that?"

They all leaned forward to squint at the blurry image of a large bird.

"The airplane?" Gabe asked.

"Wrong direction," Sean said.

"And the airplane had a solid black bird silhouette painted on the underside," Ben said. He pointed at the blurry image. "This bird has a white band around its neck."

"Assuming it's a bird at all," Sean said. "It's very blurry. I suppose it could simply be a strangely shaped cloud."

"I think it's the real Thunderbird," Tyler

whispered. "It was right there. It could have grabbed us."

"If that is a migrating bird," Sean said slowly, "It's possible it followed the other big bird in the area, namely the ultralight plane. The problem with this video, besides being blurry, is that there is nothing there for scale. We can't be sure of the bird's size. There's no way to tell."

Gabe looked at the blurry image and smiled slowly. Sure, there was no way to be sure they'd captured video of a giant bird, but they might have. As Sean ran the video over and over, Gabe hoped the huge bird got safely wherever it was going.

"You know what this means," Tyler said. "I was flying the drone and got footage of the Thunderbird." He raised both hands. "I'm king of the drone!"

ran to the ultralight to help the pilot climb out of the damaged plane. The young man blinked as they shouted questions at him.

"Are you all right?" Ben asked, taking the man's arm.

"I think so." The young man looked back at his plane and groaned. "My Thunderbird isn't."